This igloo book belongs to:

....

igloobooks

Original story by Kenneth Grahame
Retold by Stephanie Moss
Illustrated by Sumi Collina

Designed by Justine Ablett
Edited by Stephanie Moss

Copyright © 2018 Igloo Books Ltd

An imprint of Igloo Books Group,
a Bonnier Publishing company
www.bonnierpublishing.com

Published in 2018
by Igloo Books Ltd, Cottage Farm
Sywell, NN6 0BJ
All rights reserved, including the right of reproduction
in whole or in part in any form.

Manufactured in China. GUA006 0818
10 9 8 7 6 5 4 3 2 1

Library of Congress Cataloging-in-Publication
Data is available upon request.

ISBN 978-1-4998-8088-5
IglooBooks.com
www.bonnierpublishing.com

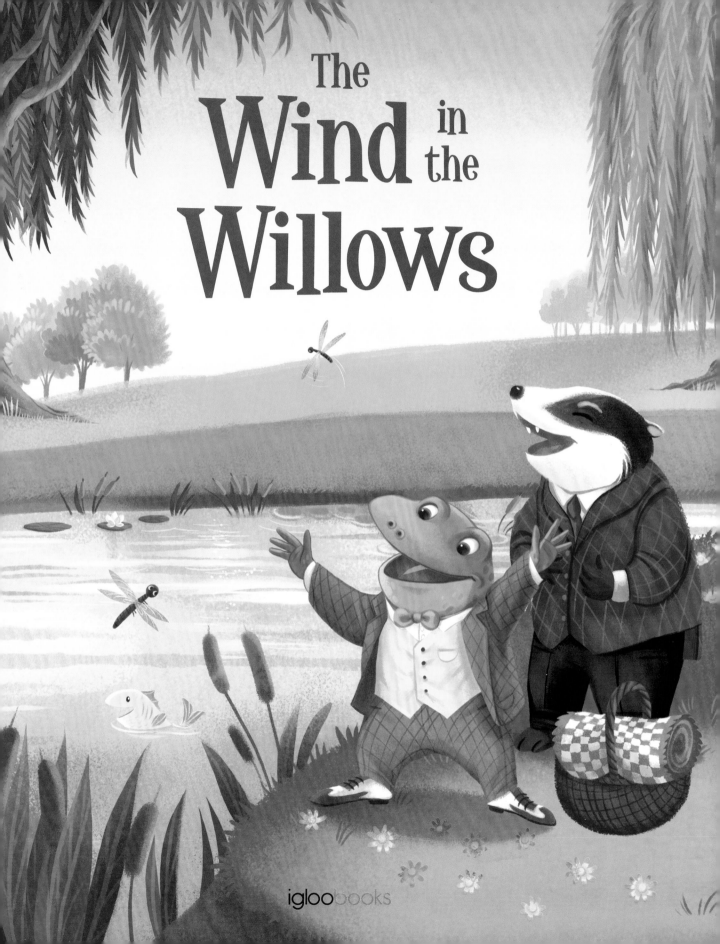

The Wind in the Willows

igloobooks

Mole lived in a gloomy underground house all by himself. One morning, he worked so hard spring-cleaning that his arms began to ache. **"I'm tired of this!"** he cried, heading out into the sunlight. He ran across meadows and by bushes, passing rabbits, birds, and beautiful flowers as he went.

Soon, Mole reached the riverbank and looked across the water. He saw a little brown face with whiskers and twinkly eyes. **"I'm Ratty,"** called the friendly creature. **"Do you want to come for a boat ride?"** Mole had never been in a boat before, so he eagerly stepped in.

"Do you ever get bored living here?" asked Mole as they rowed down the river. "No, I have lots of friends," replied Ratty. "Here's one now!" Ratty waved as Mr. Toad rowed past. "Last year, Toad loved to sail his boat," he said with a chuckle, "but now he loves rowing instead!"

Ratty docked the boat and laid out a picnic. Later, his friends Badger and Otter joined them and told stories about Mr. Toad. When it was time to go home, Ratty asked Mole, **"Would you like to come and stay with me?"** Mole was so pleased, he could hardly speak.

Ratty spent the summer teaching Mole to row and swim Then one day, Mole asked to meet Mr. Toad. **"I've heard so much about him,"** he said. So they rowed down the river until the magnificent Toad Hall appeared.

"How splendid to see you!" cried Toad, welcoming them with open arms.

Toad had forgotten all about his love of rowing and showed them his brand-new yellow wagon. **"We must take it out this afternoon!"** he cried.

"I'm not going anywhere," said Ratty, who hated leaving the river, but Toad soon convinced them to go on an adventure on the open road.

The next morning, Toad, Ratty and Mole heard a loud HONK-HONK behind the wagon. Suddenly, a speedy motorcar zoomed around the corner, leaving a cloud of dust. Their horse was so frightened, it reared up and pulled the wagon into a ditch with a crash! It fell on its side and was wrecked.

"You villains!" cried angry Ratty at the drivers, but Toad couldn't take his eyes off the disappearing vehicle. **"Are you coming to fix the wagon, Toad?"** asked Ratty.

"Oh no, I'm done with that forever!" Toad replied. The next thing they heard, Toad had bought his very own expensive motorcar.

After their adventure with Toad, winter came. Ratty spent most
of his time sleeping, so Mole went to visit Badger in the Wild Wood.
It was cold and dark there, and he saw **scary** shadows everywhere.
At last, Mole **huddled** in the hollow of an old tree and waited.

"Mole, where are you?" cried Ratty, waking up after his nap. He found Mole's footprints outside and went to look for him at once.

After hours of searching, he found his friend tired and shaking. Before they could return home, Ratty cried, **"Oh no, it's snowing!"**

The Wild Wood looked completely different. It had a gleaming white
carpet and tiny flakes filled the air. Each path looked exactly the same,
and there seemed to be no way out. The snow was so deep, Ratty and
Mole **tumbled** over on their little legs and got wet.

Suddenly, to Mole's surprise, Ratty cried,
"Look, a doormat. Hooray!"
Finally, after digging in the snow, they
found an iron bell by a dark green door.
There was a shiny, gold sign next to it.

Mr. Badger

"Come in," said Badger
when he answered the door.
"You must be freezing."

Kind Badger helped Ratty and Mole get warm and gave them a delicious dinner. Then, he asked about Toad. **"He's had seven car crashes,"** said Ratty, shaking his head. **"I'm sure he'll hurt himself again or get into more trouble."** They decided to visit Toad the next day.

When they got to Toad Hall, they saw
a brand-new, shiny motorcar.

**"Unless you promise to give up cars
forever,"** said Badger, **"we're going
to take away your keys and lock
you in your house."** Toad refused,
so his friends dragged him inside,
as he kicked and struggled.

Each animal took turns
guarding Toad until, one
morning, he asked Ratty
to fetch the doctor.
"He must be really ill,"
said Ratty. He locked
the door and ran to the
village, while sneaky Toad
hopped out of bed, made
his sheets into a rope, and
climbed out of the window

Toad marched into town. He felt very proud of himself for escaping. Suddenly, he heard a BEEP-BEEP as a car stopped nearby. No sooner had the owner gotten out than Toad found himself at the wheel, **roaring** and **racing** down the country lanes faster than ever before.

"Woo-hoo!" he cried.

It wasn't long before Toad was caught and sent to prison for stealing the car.
"Twenty years for you," said the judge, and Toad was led to the dungeon.

"Cheer up, Toad," said the guard's kind daughter, who loved animals.
"I know how you can get out of here!"

The girl helped Toad switch clothes with her aunt, who was the prison's washerwoman. Dressed in his clever disguise, Toad walked straight out of the prison gates.

"I'm free!" cried Toad, heading to the train station. He had no money for a ticket, but the kind driver gave him a ride.

Then, Toad heard shouting behind him. **"Stop, stop!"** cried a train full of policemen.

"Please save me," begged Toad. The driver tried his best, but the engine just wasn't fast enough. So Toad **jumped** from the train and hid in the woods.

In the morning, Toad brushed off the
leaves and set off for home. As he
walked by the canal, a woman on a
barge called, **"Good morning!"**
Toad, still in his washerwoman
disguise, explained that he was lost.
So the woman offered Toad a lift in
return for him washing some clothes.

The clever woman soon realized Toad was in disguise, and she flung him into the water with a great big **SPLASH!**

Toad walked back to the path, where he heard a BEEP-BEEP!
Then, he saw the very car he had stolen. He was sure he would be arrested.

Instead, the drivers believed Toad was a poor, ill washerwoman and put him in the car. **"I feel much better,"** said Toad. He added, **"Can I try driving?"** They laughed and nodded. Toad went faster and faster until he lost control and. . .

. . . CRASH!
He steered the car into the river.

The drivers and the police shouted behind Toad as the current carried him toward a dark hole in the riverbank. Then, he saw a pair of friendly eyes. **"Ratty!"** he spluttered.

"Come inside," said Ratty pulling Toad out. **"I've got something to tell you."**

The old friends talked about Toad's adventures over lunch, then Ratty began to look serious. **"You can't go home,"** he said, **"because the weasels have taken over Toad Hall."** Toad started to cry just as Badger and Mole arrived. **"Don't worry,"** said Badger. **"I have a secret plan."**

"I knew your father, Toad," explained Badger. **"He discovered a passage that goes from the riverbank, right up into Toad Hall!"** So they prepared their sticks and swords and set off into the cold, damp tunnel. They followed Badger through the darkness until they reached a trapdoor.

When the four friends peeked through the door, they saw their enemies celebrating the chief weasel's birthday in the Great Hall. Suddenly, Badger cried, **"Now!"** and the animals burst in, swishing their weapons around and yelling. The weasels were so frightened that they ran away, squeaking and squealing until none were left.

Toad planned a celebration, but Ratty made him promise to change his ways. **"You cannot spend the whole party boasting to everyone,"** he said. Toad agreed and behaved perfectly. If anyone asked about the battle with the weasels, he told them he couldn't have done it without his friends.

The party was a great success and Toad's friends found he had changed
for good. He even made a promise to find and repay anyone that he
had ever wronged! From that very day on, Toad, Ratty, Mole, and Badger
lived peacefully along the beautiful riverside together.

Discover all eight enchanting classic tales...

Alice in Wonderland

Join Alice and tumble down the rabbit hole into Wonderland, where nothing is as it seems. This beautiful book is perfect for creating the most magical of story times for every little reader.

Black Beauty

Rediscover this moving story of one horse's trials and hardships in this classic tale. When Black Beauty grows to be a handsome stallion, he is passed from one owner to the next, but will he ever be free?

The Jungle Book

Join Mowgli as he learns the strange ways of the jungle, guided wisely by Baloo the bear. This retelling of the timeless classic, with beautiful illustrations, will capture every child's imagination.

Oliver Twist

Dive into the life of pickpocketing crooks in this captivating tale. Follow poor little orphan Oliver all the way from the workhouse until he meets Fagin's gang. Can he escape the streets?

The Secret Garden

Unlock the door to a magical place, full of beauty and mystery. Mary Lennox is lonely and spoiled, but when she discovers a garden hidden in the grounds, it will change her family forever.

Treasure Island

Set sail on a rip-roaring adventure in this classic tale of swashbuckling pirates and hidden treasure. This exciting tale, with stunning original illustrations, is perfect for a thrilling story time.

The Wind in the Willows

Join Mole and his friends for a riverbank adventure in this classic tale of friendship. Can Mole, Ratty, and Badger keep the mischievous Mr. Toad out of trouble? Find out in this beautiful, timeless classic.

The Wizard of Oz

Be swept away with Dorothy and Toto to the Land of Oz, where they meet Scarecrow, Tin Man, and Lion. This retelling of the well-loved classic story is sure to make story time exciting.